THE SOMEDAY HOUSE

A RICHARD JACKSON BOOK

THE SOMEDAY HOUSE

BY ANNE SHELBY
ILLUSTRATED BY ROSANNE LITZINGER

ORCHARD BOOKS / NEW YORK

Orchard Books, 95 Madison Avenue, New York, NY 10016

Manufactured in the United States of America. Printed by Barton Press, Inc. Bound by Horowitz/Rae. Book design by Jean Krulis. The text of this book is set in 28 point Leawood Book. The illustrations are gouache on Arches watercolor paper.

1   3   5   7   9   10   8   6   4   2

Library of Congress Cataloging-in-Publication Data. Shelby, Anne. Someday house / by Anne Shelby ; illustrated by Rosanne Litzinger. p. cm. "A Richard Jackson book"—Half t.p. Summary: Describes what it would be like to live in a house on a mountain, by the sea, above a bakery, underground, and in other wonderful places. ISBN 0-531-09510-X. — ISBN 0-531-08860-X (lib. bdg.) [1. Dwellings—Fiction.] I. Litzinger, Rosanne, ill.   II. Title.   PZ7.S54125So   1996   [E]—dc20   95-23178

Someday we'll live
in a house on a mountain.
We'll sit on the roof
and fill the sky with bubbles.

Someday we'll live
in a house by the sea
so we can hear the ocean sing
and play tag with the waves.

Someday we'll live
on a houseboat on a river.

We'll move every day
and never have to pack.

Someday we'll live
next door
to a family band
and dance
when they play music
on their porch.

Someday we'll live
above a bakery.
We'll help the baker clean the place
and collect our pay in pies.

Someday we'll live
in a house underground
where we'll be cool in summer,
safe from storms…

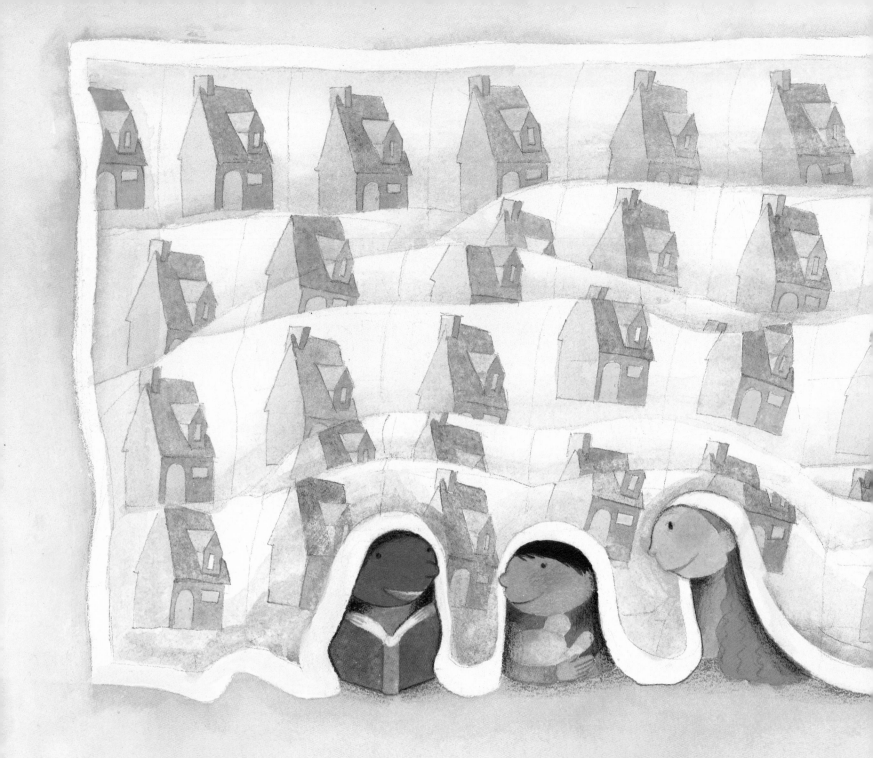

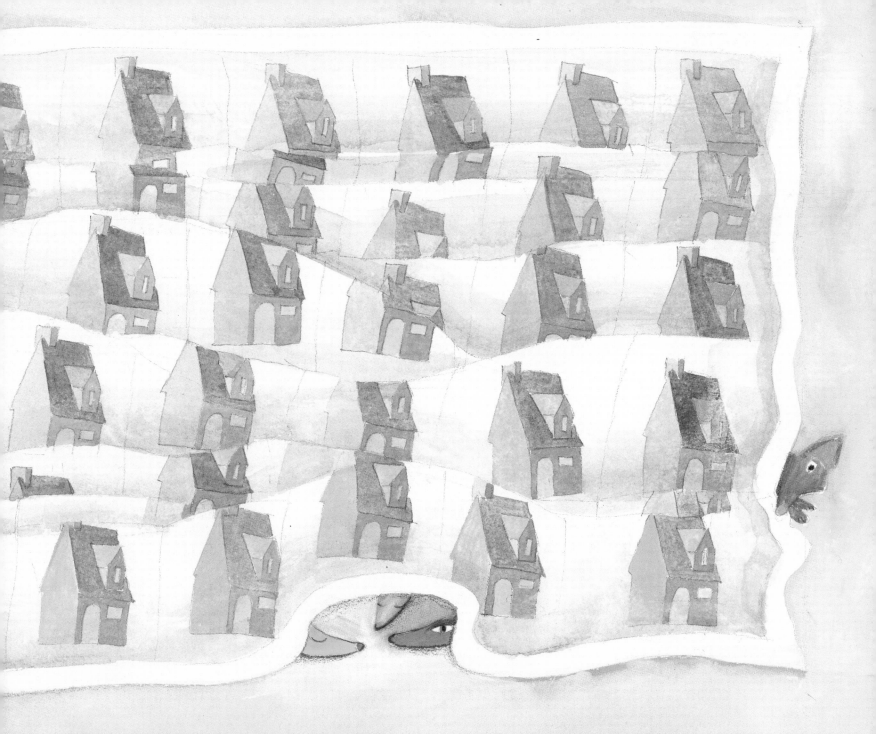

and snug as bugs when snow flies overhead.

Someday we'll live
in a house with a secret passage,

perfect
for hide–and–go–seek.

Someday we'll live
in a house of living trees.

We'll hang wind chimes in every room
and we won't need steps
to climb upstairs.

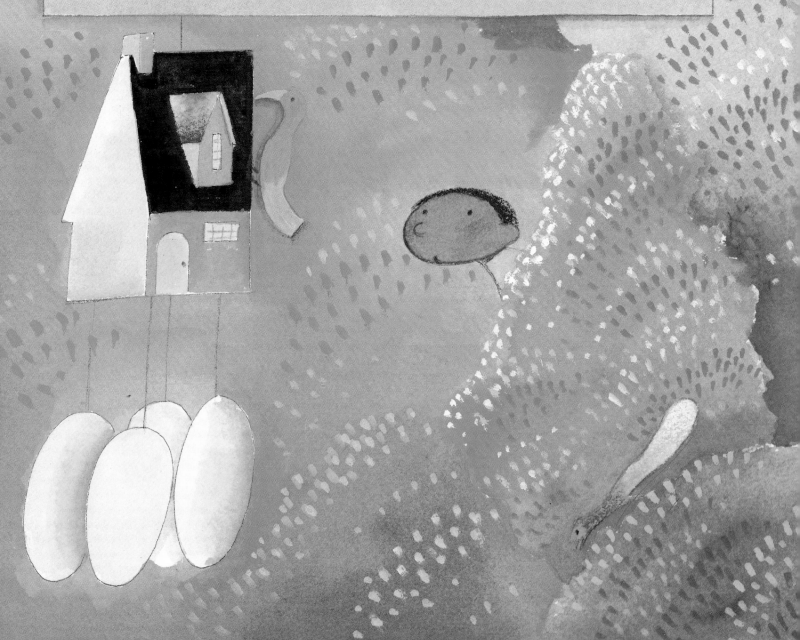

Someday we'll live
in a house shaped like an "O"
with a fine flat roof for roller skating.

Someday we'll live
in a house in space.

Our yard will be
out   of   this   world.

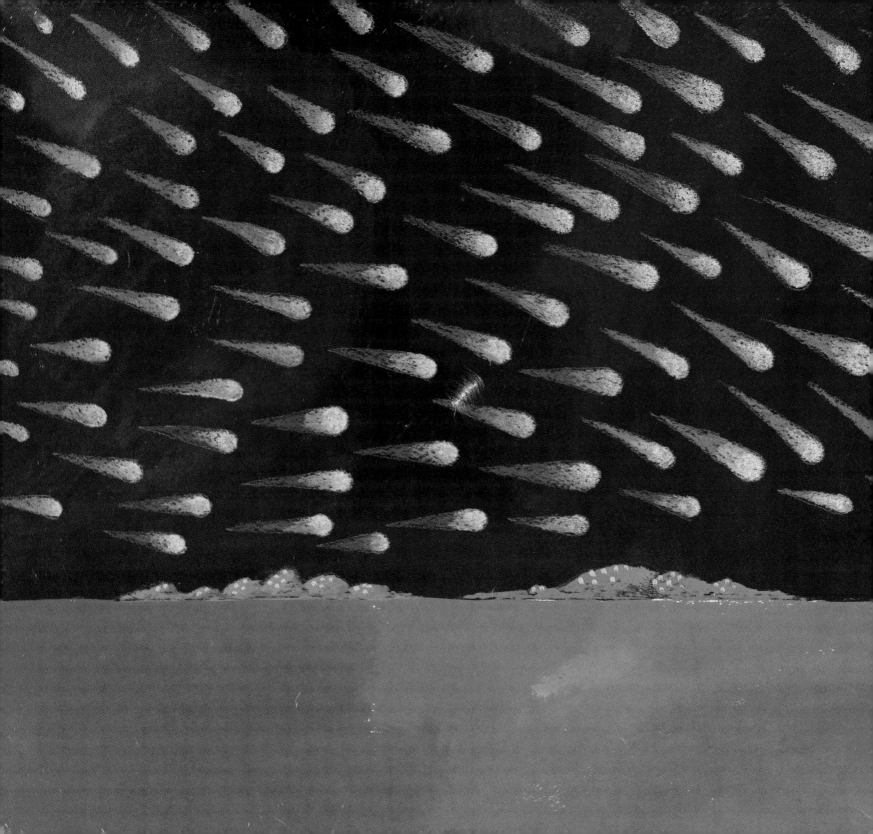

Someday we'll live...

in a house with a hundred rooms.
We can always build on
if we need more.